TEEN LIFE 411™

I HAVE BEEN RAPED.
NOW WHAT?

SUSAN HENNEBERG

ROSEN
PUBLISHING®

New York

Published in 2016 by The Rosen Publishing Group, Inc.
29 East 21st Street, New York, NY 10010

Copyright © 2016 by The Rosen Publishing Group, Inc.

First Edition

Library of Congress Cataloging-in-Publication Data

Henneberg, Susan.
I have been raped. Now what?/Susan Henneberg.—
First edition.
    pages cm.—(Teen life 411)
Includes bibliographical references and index.
ISBN 978-1-4994-6142-8 (library bound)
1. Rape—Juvenile literature. 2. Rape victims—Juvenile literature. 3. Rape victims—Services for—Juvenile literature.
I. Title.
HV6558.H435 2016
362.8830835'2—dc23
                                                    2014040076

Manufactured in the United States of America

For many of the images in this book, the people photographed are models. The depictions do not imply actual situations or events.

CONTENTS

It was an unimaginable act of violence. On August 11, 2012, two Steubenville, Ohio, high school football players raped a sixteen-year-old girl from West Virginia. For over six hours, they repeatedly assaulted the girl, who had passed out from drinking alcohol. Then they, and other witnesses, posted photos and videos of the assault on social media and in text messages to friends.

The crime tore apart the town. Two of the boys charged with the rape were convicted. One was sentenced to one year in juvenile detention. The other was sentenced to two years in detention. Several of the adults who protected the offenders were brought up on criminal charges. Classmates threatened the victim on Twitter. Some media commentators sympathized with the offenders. The tragic ordeal didn't end there for the victim. Her name was released on national television.

The statistics on teen rape are sobering. According to a 2010 survey conducted by the Centers for

People protested against Steubenville's law enforcement agencies. They claimed that they attempted to cover up the rape.

Disease Control and Prevention (CDC), nearly one in five women and one in seventy-one men have been raped in their lifetimes. Almost half of them experienced their first rape before age eighteen. Teens who identify as lesbian, gay, and bisexual experience equal or higher rates of sexual violence. Only three out of every one hundred rapists will ever go to jail, according to an analysis of Justice Department data done by the Rape, Abuse & Incest National Network (RAINN).

Survivors of rape and sexual assault say victims often never recover from the nightmare. They feel shame and guilt. They experience physical, psychological, and social consequences. They may suffer from post-traumatic stress disorder (PTSD). They get depressed, develop sleep disorders, and find it difficult to resume normal life. They sometimes engage in behaviors such as using drugs, cutting, or overeating. In two recent well-publicized cases, the victims committed suicide.

You, or someone you know, may be a victim of rape or sexual assault. You may be male or female, live in wealth or in poverty. You may be an A student or a dropout. You may have told the police or a trusted adult, or you may still be suffering in silence. Whatever your circumstances, those who have survived rape, and those who have helped the survivors, have two very important messages for you. The first one is that no matter how much you had to drink, what you wore, or what you did before the assault, it is not your fault. If you are under the age of consent or you did not give clear consent to have sex, it is rape.

New York residents were outraged when a judge dismissed charges that a prominent French economist sexually assaulted a hotel maid in 2011.

The second message from rape survivors is that you do not have to endure this trauma alone. If you are courageous enough to tell someone, there is a whole community ready to help you find your way back to wholeness. You may choose to stay silent and try to recover on your own. However, most rape victims say that the support they received from family, friends, law enforcement, rape counselors, and the criminal justice system made all the difference in being able to move on with their lives. Learning as much as you can about the causes and effects of rape may help you and your community prevent future rapes. Rapists can be brought to justice. Victims can eventually heal.

CHAPTER 1

Every two minutes, someone in the United States is raped, reports RAINN. Almost half of the victims are eighteen or younger. One in ten rape victims is male. Ninety-three percent of teen victims know their attacker. Teens are raped by family members, coaches, school friends and acquaintances, and their boyfriends.

Rape is a traumatic experience no matter what the age of the victim. For teens, it can be devastating. They are overwhelmed by emotions. They may be physically injured. They have to make adult decisions such as whom to tell, whether to go to the hospital, or whether to call the police. After the rape, they may still have to see their attackers every day.

Maybe you know someone who was raped. She may have told you but didn't tell her mother. According to a 2007 Utah survey, 70 percent of teens told a friend about their rape, compared to 12 percent who told a parent. She probably didn't report it. Only 40 percent of victims notify the police about the assault, according to RAINN. Male victims report less frequently than females. Your friend might have been intoxicated. The National Institute on Alcohol and Alcoholism estimates that half of all teen perpetrators and half of all teen sexual assault victims had been drinking to excess.

You may notice that the rape victim's behavior changed after the rape. He may act withdrawn and quiet. She may act depressed, skip school, and withdraw from friends. Victims may be harassed on Facebook or Twitter, especially if there are cell phone photos. Victims' physical wounds may heal, but they don't "get over it." They often can't seem to put the event behind them.

This was the case for fifteen-year-old Audrie Pott, a sophomore at Saratoga High School in Northern California. In the beginning of the 2012 school year, she had gone to a party at a friend's house whose parents were away. She drank alcohol mixed with Gatorade. According to a 2013 *Rolling Stone* article, everyone at the party, including Audrie, was "trashed." Several boys

Audrie Pott's parents worked to pass a cyberbullying law after photos of their daughter's rape were posted on social media.

took her upstairs to a bedroom and removed her clothes. They wrote all over her with Sharpies and then took cell phone photos. They then raped her with their fingers.

When Audrie woke up the next morning, she called her mom to pick her up. Before long, the story was all over her school. She put on a brave face, but friends noticed by the marks on her arms that she had begun cutting. Only two weeks after the party, Audrie couldn't take the humiliation anymore. She hanged herself in her bathroom. In 2013, two boys at her school were convicted of raping her at the party and texting cell phone photos of the assault to their friends.

Not every rape case involving teens follows this scenario. Boys are raped by their coaches in the locker room after practice. Young girls are sexually assaulted by their stepfathers or stepbrothers. Seven percent of the time the rapist is a total stranger who finds a victim alone and vulnerable.

WHAT IS RAPE?

The word "rape" comes from a very old word that means "to seize, to carry off." The U.S. Department of Justice's meaning is far more brutal. The DOJ defines it as "penetration, no matter how slight, of the vagina or anus with any body part or object, or oral penetration by a sex organ of another person, without the consent of the victim." Victims of rape understand the origin of the word. They feel as if their innocence has been seized and carried off by their rapists.

The way different states define rape can be confusing. In some states, rape and sexual assault are the same crime. In other states, there are different categories. For example, North Carolina uses the word "rape" for vaginal penetration. Sexual assault refers to "a sexual act," such as oral sex or penetration using fingers or objects. Rape or sexual assault in the first degree means that a deadly weapon was used or the victim was seriously injured. The term "second degree" means that the victim did not consent to intercourse. If the victim was mentally or physically incapacitated, he or she cannot give consent. Someone who is under the influence of drugs or alcohol is considered physically incapacitated. Most states have similar laws.

STATUTORY RAPE

The word "statutory" means pertaining to state law. These laws refer to sexual intercourse with a person who is considered too young to give consent. These laws protect children and young teens from older predators. In these cases, it doesn't matter if the young person gives consent. He or she is considered not mature enough to make that decision.

Statutory rape laws are different in each state. The punishments depend on the age of the victim and the age of the offender. The younger the victim, and the older the offender, the longer the prison sentence. For instance, in Arizona, if the victim is under twelve but the offender is at least eighteen, the punishment is life

CAN A GUY BE RAPED?

A CDC 2011 survey found that 4.5 percent of boys from grades nine through twelve reported that they were forced to have sexual intercourse at some time in their lives. Most of the perpetrators were known to the boys. Most of the perpetrators were not homosexual. Some were women who enjoy taking advantage of boys. One myth about male rape is that if the victim gets an erection, he enjoyed the assault. The reality is that sexual stimulation is likely to happen in a sexual situation. It does not mean the boy or man wanted the experience. Being sexually assaulted by a man does not mean that a boy is homosexual. It does mean that he will likely suffer as many negative physical and emotional effects as girls who are assaulted.

Teacher Mary Kay LeTourneau went to prison for having sex with one of her twelve-year-old male students. Her act is considered statutory rape.

in prison. If the victim is between twelve and fourteen, and the offender is at least eighteen, the punishment is twenty years. If the victim is at least fifteen, the sentence is one year in prison. All states set the age of consent between fourteen and eighteen, with most at age sixteen. Most states reserve the harshest punishments for offenders over twenty-one.

DIFFERENT KINDS OF RAPE

Rape is unfortunately a common crime in the United States. RAINN estimates that one out of every six American women will become a victim of rape or attempted rape. There are many different circumstances in which rape occurs. The most common type of rape is date or acquaintance rape. This rape happens in a social situation where one person forces another person to have intercourse without consent. The CDC estimates that almost two-thirds of teen rapes are date rapes. When a rape occurs in a social situation and the victim is attacked by a group of people, it is called gang rape. The offenders in this type of rape are often young men who are in a group together. For instance, they may be friends from the same school, play on a sports team, belong to a college fraternity, or belong to a criminal gang.

The second most common type of rape is sexual assault among family members. When this occurs between close blood members, such as father and daughter, it is called incest. RAINN estimates that about one-third of children and teen rapes are by family members. Close family friends can also intimidate children into becoming rape victims. Three-time Tour de France winner Greg LeMond kept his childhood sexual abuse by a family friend secret until well into his adulthood. Rape can even happen in a marriage. If one spouse forces sex on the other without his or her consent, it is spousal rape.

Mentor rape occurs when a person who acts as a trusted adviser sexually assaults the person he or she is mentoring. This person can be a coach, youth group adviser, or pastor. One high-profile example of this type of rape is the case of Pennsylvania State University assistant football coach Jerry Sandusky. In 2012, he was found guilty of molesting children who participated in his organization for at-risk children. Custodial rape happens when someone who is not a family member but has custody of a child assaults the child. This could occur in a foster

College football coach Jerry Sandusky was sentenced to life imprisonment for the sexual abuse of young boys. He met the boys through his work at a charity for at-risk youth.

home. Prison rape occurs when a prison guard rapes an inmate or inmates rape other inmates. The DOJ estimates that 12 percent of youth in juvenile facilities are sexually assaulted by another youth or facility staff.

Rape in the military is receiving a lot more attention than it used to. In 2013, the U.S. Commission

Military victims of sexual assault have testified in Congress. They are calling for better care and treatment for soldiers who have been raped or assaulted by other members of the military.

MS. SANDERS

on Civil Rights reported that 23 percent of women and 4 percent of men reported experiencing unwanted sexual contact after their enlistment. Over half of this contact was rape. Another type of rape, war rape, is rare in the United States but is common in some parts of the world. According to the United Nations, "rape is used as a weapon to terrorize individual women and girls, and also to terrorize their families and to terrorize entire communities." Rape as a weapon of war has occurred in Rwanda, Sudan, and the Democratic Republic of Congo, all in Africa.

WHAT CONSENT MEANS

"Consent" means clearly agreeing to have sex. It means that both partners are considered old enough by state law to have sex. It means that both partners have the capacity to consent. Neither has been drinking or abusing drugs. It means that both

MS. WILI

Veteran

partners agreed to take part. One is not threatening to humiliate or physically hurt the other if he or she refuses. A no can be communicated nonverbally, such as a push or attempt to leave. Both people must be conscious and willing participants.

There are many misconceptions about rape and consent. Some people believe that if a person doesn't resist physically, it isn't rape. However, some victims may decide that resisting may make the attacker become more violent. Some may think that if a person is too intoxicated or high to give consent, then it isn't rape. Most state laws say that an intoxicated person cannot give consent. Some teens think that if they have given consent before, then it isn't rape. According to the law, both partners have to give clear consent every time they are asked to have sex. Otherwise it is rape.

Many rape situations are very complex. Teens become confused and overwhelmed by sexual assault from family members, especially if it begins in childhood. In dating

Columbia University student Emma Sulkowicz carries a mattress around campus to call attention to the university's lack of response to her alleged rape.

relationships, many teens are sexually inexperienced and don't communicate well. They are also unfamiliar with the effects of alcohol. These are some reasons why most rapes are not reported. When they are reported, very few offenders are convicted of a crime.

Almost everyone will want a mature sexual relationship in his or her adult life. That is why it is important to be very clear about what constitutes healthy, legal sexual experiences. Responsible teens need to learn what is or isn't rape and the importance of giving consent.

CHAPTER 2

Although violent crime, including rape, has been decreasing over the last decade, we still live in a society where far too many people become victims of sexual violence. Many experts believe that we live in a rape culture. They claim that our society excuses and even encourages male sexual aggression. Alcohol, pornography, date rape drugs, and popular music all play a role in causing sexual assault.

RAPE CULTURE

Beginning in childhood, we are surrounded by stereotypes that teach boys and girls how to behave toward each other. Stereotypes are commonly held beliefs that may or may not be true. Boys are often brought up to enjoy sports and to play them aggressively. They are given G.I. Joes and guns to play with. They learn to fight with their fists to solve conflicts. They play video games in which their characters use violence to win. The females in these games are "damsels in distress" who need to be rescued by the strong males.

Boys who watch sports on TV see commercials in which women are sexual objects used to sell products. They listen to rap music that contains references to sexual violence. They learn when they start dating that men should

make the first phone call. On a date, they make the first moves. In team locker rooms, college fraternity houses, and street gangs, young men reinforce each other's sexual aggressiveness.

Girls are raised with different expectations. They are given dolls to play with. They are expected to be nurturing and emotional. The messages they see—from greeting cards to popular magazines—teach them to be passive and weak. They find it hard to clearly state their needs and wants because the desires of men have always come first. Decades of watching strong women compete in sports and decisive

Young women in sexy outfits are used to attract the attention of male consumers, especially for products such as beer and sports cars.

women lead cities, states, and nations have not yet overcome generations of belief about the limits of women. This perceived helplessness of women sometimes makes them easy to be victimized.

Both young men and women are given mixed messages when it comes to dating and sex. Girls are expected to play "hard to get." They are called trashy or worse if they wear short skirts or low-cut blouses. If they are sexually assaulted, they are accused of "asking for it." Yet teen fashion magazines and stores promote clothes that are very revealing. Girls hear a message that says that acting and dressing sexy is the way to be popular, especially with boys. A 2014 song by pop singer Meghan Trainor says, "I can shake it, shake it like I'm supposed to do/'Cause I got that boom boom that all the boys chase." Girls often believe the stereotype that says they are objects for men's pleasure.

Young men receive mixed messages as well. They are taught to respect women by opening doors for them and paying for their dinners. They are told that part of the game of "hard to get" is that a woman's no really means "yes, but I need to be persuaded first." The music that guys listen to implies that sex and violence go together. Young teen listeners use this music to figure out how to act in sexual situations. They learn about hypermasculinity. This is an exaggeration of male traits, such as being aggressive and demanding.

Rap music has often been accused of being misogynistic. This means that the lyrics and videos support the idea that women are objects to be exploited by men. Songs often use derogatory names for women, talk about violence toward them, and glorify prostitution. Rap music critic James Peterson, in the book *Sexual Violence*, quotes a study showing that 64 percent of rap lyrics have degrading sexual content toward women. He thinks that rap artists use such lyrics to prove that they are "authentic gangsters." The music both reflects and shapes a misogynistic culture.

RAP'S RAPE CULTURE

Hip-hop music often sends a message to listeners that women should be treated as sex objects and prizes for men who become successful.

THE IMPACT OF ALCOHOL AND DRUGS ON TEEN RAPE

Kierra Johnson was just fifteen when she cut school one day to drink vodka with three boys from her school. As she drifted in and out of consciousness, the boys raped her. She never got to see the sentencing of her rapists, who were given from six to twelve years in jail. She died at the scene of the rape from alcohol poisoning. According to a 2010 *Philadelphia Daily News* article, the boys will have to register as sex offenders for the rest of their lives.

Very few rapes end in the death of the victim. Experts estimate that almost half of all rapes are associated with alcohol. They aren't sure of the exact number because of many factors. First, most sexual assaults are not reported. Teen victims may feel that they will be punished for admitting to drinking alcohol. They may think that because they were intoxicated, they were responsible for the rape. Because of the intoxication, the participants may not remember much about the event.

Researchers from the National Institute of Alcohol Abuse and Alcoholism looked at the connection between rape and alcohol. They found that rape involving alcohol most often occurred between men and women who did not know each other very well. The assaults happened during social interactions, such as parties. The men in the studies reported that alcohol gave them "liquid courage." Alcohol disrupted the parts of their brains that determined consequences for their actions. The researchers found that intoxicated women were less able to physically resist assault. Alcohol makes both men and women less able to communicate effectively about how far they want the sexual encounter to go. It also makes them take more risks.

PORNOGRAPHY AND RAPE

There was a time when teens who wanted to view pornography had to sneak looks at their fathers' magazines. Now violent and degrading photos and videos are available on their smartphones twenty-four hours a day, sometimes for free. A 2013 survey reported in the *Journal of Sex Research* found that 85 percent of adolescent boys and 42 percent of girls watched pornography, some as much as fifty times. This same journal article found that in the majority of videos advertising themselves as having "teen" subjects, the female actors in the beginning showed reluctance to have sex. However, they were quickly persuaded and ended up enjoying the sexual activity they had originally resisted. The journal authors called this token resistance. According to the authors, token resistance is defined as when people on a date, usually women, say no when they mean yes and their protests are not to be taken seriously. The authors found that more frequent viewing of pornography is associated with stronger beliefs in token resistance.

Internet-connected technology such as smartphones have made it easy to find and watch pornography, often for free. Teens and young men are the biggest consumers of Internet porn.

Author Todd Kendall, quoting a *Scientific American* article in his chapter in the book *Sexual Violence*, found that access to pornography was associated with decreased rape. The rate of men watching porn, thanks to the Internet, has gone up. At the same time, the rate of rape has gone down. He thinks that watching porn may be a substitute for sexual assault for some men. Both writers agree that more research needs to be done to clarify the connection between pornography and rape.

DATE RAPE DRUGS

The number-one date rape drug is alcohol. Marijuana, LSD, ecstasy, and other street drugs, as well as prescription drugs such as OxyContin and Vicodin, act in similar ways as alcohol in terms of affecting judgment and lowering inhibitions. In excess, they can make victims too physically helpless to refuse sex.

Most date rape drugs are sedatives originally developed to help sleep disorders. They became popular at clubs and raves. They are powerful and dangerous. Rohypnol, also known as roofies, ropies, circles, or trip-and-fall, is illegal in the United States. It is a small blue pill that makes drinks turn blue or cloudy. Victims of this drug look and act intoxicated. They often lose consciousness. Usually they don't remember what happened while they were drugged.

GHB, also known as liquid ecstasy, liquid X, cherry meth, or gamma 10, comes in a liquid or powder form. It tastes slightly salty. Victims feel intoxicated, dizzy, and sleepy. An overdose can cause seizures, coma, and death.

Ketamine, also known as special K, vitamin K, or kit kat, comes as a liquid or white powder. It can cause hallucinations, euphoria, delusions, aggressive behavior, and numbness. It can make a victim's heart race.

There are many reasons why these drugs are used by sexual predators. The drugs are mostly tasteless, odorless, and colorless. They are easily slipped into drinks and fast acting. They make the victim passive and incapable of thinking clearly. The drugs are hard to spot in a routine toxicology screen or blood test. Doctors and police have to be specifically looking for the drugs and work fast to find them in a victim's body.

Sexual predators can more easily drug women who do not keep a close eye on their drinks. Alcohol is the most common date rape drug.

The most important way to avoid becoming a victim of a date rape drug is to stay aware of everything happening to you. These drugs are most often slipped into alcoholic drinks, so sticking with soft drinks will help keep you safe. If you do drink alcohol, don't accept drinks from other people. Open containers yourself. Keep your drink with you at all times. Don't drink out of punchbowls. Stay with a nondrinking friend. If you feel you are losing control too quickly, call for help immediately.

Teens today live in a sexualized society. The music they listen to, the movies they watch, and the clothes advertised to them all send mixed messages about sexuality. On the one hand, girls are harassed if they dress in low-cut or tight clothing and told to be vigilant about date rape drugs. Yet sex is marketed in pop songs and fashion magazines, and alcohol is everywhere. Boys are raised to treat women with respect. Yet pop culture urges them to act forcefully and aggressively in demanding sex. It is no wonder that teens are often confused about the sexual expectations of their world.

MYTH

Someone who dresses in a sexy way is asking to be raped.

FACT

People who dress in a sexy way enjoy the way they look. They are not asking to have sex against their will.

MYTH

If a person didn't fight back, he or she wasn't raped.

FACT

People forced to have sex against their will were raped, whether or not they made the choice to fight back.

MYTH

Men who rape other men are gay.

FACT

The vast majority of men who rape other men are heterosexual. They are acting on violent, not sexual, urges.

MYTHS AND FACTS

CHAPTER 3

WHAT TO DO IF IT HAPPENS TO YOU

Writer Neesha Arter was fourteen when she was raped by two boys, one of whom she'd secretly had a crush on. In her 2013 *Teen Vogue* article, she describes the experience this way:

> My body felt so heavy, my muscles so weak. I used every bit of strength I had to pull myself away, but it wasn't enough. Their hands overpowered me and I couldn't break free. I closed my lips and bit them as hard as I could. Staring into the boys' eyes I thought were so beautiful just a few moments before, I wanted to be somewhere far, far away. My blood was boiling, my skin sweating; all of this seemed like a fever-induced hallucination. Two salty tears began to stream down my face.
>
> And then two hundred tears.

Rape can happen to anyone. No one expects to be assaulted. Very few victims know what to do when an assault happens to them. Scared, possibly hurt, humiliated, they often are hesitant to call the police. They don't want family or friends to know. The steps victims take after a rape, however, can determine some important outcomes. Getting medical treatment can help preserve valuable evidence of the crime. Reporting the crime to the police can help bring the rapist to justice. Talking to a rape crisis counselor can start the process of recovery.

THE FIRST STEPS

Most crime victims report that they are so over-whelmed after the crime, they can't think clearly. Time is very important after a rape, however. You may need treatment after an assult. You need to preserve possible DNA evidence, such as skin under fingernails and semen on clothing. You need medical professionals to get a urine sample or blood test if you think you have been drugged. You need to involve law enforcement while you can accurately recall the details of the assault.

RAINN says that the first step is to find a safe location away from the perpetrator. Then you need to find a trusted friend or family member to help with the next steps. If the assault occurred late at night, this may be difficult. You may be stranded at a party miles away from home. Or you may be in a parking lot or on the street. In a dangerous situation, calling 911 is the best option. When you talk to the emergency dispatcher, you can ask for a representative from a rape crisis center to be available wherever you are taken.

Male victims are often reluctant to call for help. They blame themselves for the assault. They believe that they were not strong enough to fight off the perpetrator. They may be confused that they became physically aroused during the attack, though these responses in no way imply they enjoyed the attack. Victims can remain anonymous when calling a sexual assault hotline.

SEEKING MEDICAL TREATMENT

RAINN advises that rape victims go to a hospital for a forensic medical exam. One purpose of the exam is to collect evidence of the rape. Teens need to know that medical professionals such as doctors and nurses are mandatory reporters. If you are under eighteen, they will have to notify law enforcement about a suspected rape. Until you have the exam, RAINN says that you should not bathe or shower, brush your teeth, use the restroom, change

Nurses can take special training to conduct forensic sexual assault exams through a sexual assault nurse examiner (SANE) training program.

clothes, comb your hair, or clean up the crime scene. Refraining from these actions will improve the chances that police can access and test evidence at a later date.

At the hospital, especially in larger communities, you might be examined by a sexual assault nurse examiner (SANE) or a sexual assault forensic examiner (SAFE). These medical professionals are specially trained to offer victims compassionate care while finding and preserving evidence. They understand the trauma you have gone through and will patiently lead you through what may be a lengthy exam.

The examining doctor or nurse will first write down a detailed medical history. Next, there will be a complete exam. This may be unpleasant. You already feel as if your body has been invaded. Now a medical professional wants to swab your orifices and take photos of your private parts and bruised areas. This procedure is part of what is called a rape kit. The examiners are looking for hair, semen, saliva, and fibers that can be used as evidence. The kit itself is a large envelope or box, which can store the evidence collected from your body or clothing. The hospital should inform you how long they will keep the kit and what they will do with it when that time is up.

The doctor or nurse will offer you postexposure prophylaxis (PEP). PEP is preventative medical treatment immediately after exposure to disease-causing viruses, such as HIV. They may treat you for other sexually transmitted infections. They may offer emergency

Rape kits are important sources of evidence if victims choose to press charges against the perpetrators of the rape. The kit contains hair, semen, fibers, and saliva collected from the victim.

contraception to prevent pregnancy or tell you where to obtain it. They should explain the reasons for everything they do in terms you understand. If you haven't before, this is the time to ask for a rape crisis counselor or victim advocate, who can help you make decisions.

As a victim of sexual assault, you have several rights at the hospital. You can refuse any or all parts of the exam. Under the Violence Against Women and Department of Justice Reauthorization Act of 2005, states have to provide the exam free of charge or with full reimbursement if you do get charged. States can't put conditions on the free exam, such as your cooperation with law enforcement officials.

Sexual Assault Nurse Examiners (SANE)

A SANE is a registered nurse who has had training and certification in the forensic examination of sexual assault victims. This means that they are specialists in collecting evidence for more effective investigations and better prosecutions. They offer prompt, empathetic care to overwhelmed victims. SANE programs can be coordinated by hospitals, rape crisis centers, or law enforcement. These nurses are most often available twenty-four hours a day.

Why Reporting Rape Is Important

If you decide not to go to the hospital or call law enforcement, your chances of bringing the rapist to justice are drastically reduced. You may decide just to keep the whole event a secret. Experts in the mental health field say concealment is not a good idea. Your family and friends would not want or expect you to keep such a traumatic secret. They will understand that this assault was not your fault. The emotional reactions you may be experiencing can affect you for many years. Friends and family can provide the support you need to heal.

Calling just one nationwide hotline can connect you to a local rape crisis center. The person who answers your call can provide answers to your questions.

You can call a rape crisis center for rape counseling. On the phone, you can remain anonymous while you talk about the event. Calling one number in the United States, 1-800-656-HOPE (4673), will connect you with the nearest rape crisis center. If you are under eighteen and share your name with the rape crisis counselor, most states consider him or her a mandatory reporter. You may have a good relationship with a school counselor, teacher, or church minister; they are also mandatory reporters. If you are a minor, they will have to inform the police about the assault.

If you do not get medical care after your rape, you need to be aware that you might have been exposed to sexually transmitted diseases (STDs). A fever, a rash, blisters, itching, abdominal pain, vaginal discharge, redness, swelling, burning in the vaginal area, and pelvic cramping are all symptoms that need to be checked out by a doctor. If you were subjected to an oral assault, you need to watch for mouth or throat ulcers, rash, pain, or blisters. Some STDs, such as chlamydia and HIV, do not have immediate symptoms. If you do contract an STD and do not treat it, you can infect any sexual partners you have after the rape.

Both male and female victims of sexual assault need to be checked out for STDs. Females need to also be concerned about pregnancy. There is about a 5 percent chance that a rape victim will become pregnant. Emergency contraception pills (ECPs) are available in pharmacies. In many states, teens need to be at least seventeen to buy them without a prescription. If you are younger than seventeen, you will need a doctor's prescription. One brand, Plan B One Step, has been approved by the U.S. Food and

Drug Administration (FDA) to be sold over the counter without a prescription or age requirement. The pill needs to be taken within five days of the rape. Side effects might include nausea, vomiting, breast tenderness, abdominal pain, headache, dizziness, and fatigue. They usually last only a few days.

Plan B is an emergency contraception pill (ECP) that does not require a prescription. ECPs can prevent pregnancy after sexual intercourse. Girls who are sexually active should talk to their doctors about regular contraceptive methods, however.

The 2007 Utah survey found that only 20 percent of rape victims sought medical care after their assault. Other statistics from the survey showed low access of resources that might be useful after such a traumatic event. Only 3 percent contacted a sexual assault or rape crisis phone line. Fourteen percent were reported to the police. States and local communities are stepping forward with resources and processes that make reporting of sexual assault safer, more protective, and more productive.

CHAPTER 4

Rape is one of the most terrifying crimes that can happen to someone. If it happened to you, you most likely became overwhelmed with not only the event itself but also with the important decisions you needed to make afterward. You had to decide whether to go to the hospital to get treated. The next decision is whether to report the crime to the police. Hopefully, you took advantage of offers from family, medical professionals, and victims' advocates from the nearest rape crisis center to help you make these decisions.

REPORTING TO THE POLICE

After a traumatizing sexual assault, you may not want to contact the police. You may not be ready to answer a lot of questions about the rape, reliving every detail. However, RAINN encourages you to take this important step. The organization says, "While there's no way to change what happened to you, you can seek justice while helping to stop [a rape] from happening to someone else." Though it is your decision to make, prosecuting the rapist is an effective tool to prevent future rapes.

There might be several reasons you may not want to contact the police. You may think that police officers might not believe you, especially if there are no physical injuries. Disbelief is rarely the case. Law enforcement officers are trained to investigate every crime that is reported. Some police departments have sexual assault response teams (SARTs) that respond to reports of rapes with sensitivity.

You may think that the officers will accuse you of causing the rape by wearing suggestive clothing, going out drinking with the perpetrator, or agreeing to make out with him. Victim blaming occurred in what is called the Roast Buster scandal in New Zealand. The Roast Busters are a group of young men accused of gang-raping underaged girls and then boasting about the crimes on Facebook. One young girl said in an interview that she didn't have a case because the police said she was wearing clothes that were "pretty much asking for it."

Holly Mullen, executive director of the Salt Lake City, Utah, Rape Recovery Center (RRC) said in a May 29, 2014, RRC blog post, "We spend an inordinate amount

Girls who wear sexually suggestive clothes and flirt with young men want to have fun. They are never asking to be sexually assaulted.

of time with our clients trying to reverse this [blame the victim] mentality among victims and our entire society. Short skirts and bare arms do not cause rape. Rapists cause rape." If you were assaulted, you need to understand that you did not cause the rape; you are not at fault.

You may not want to report it because you are afraid of getting into trouble. Maybe you snuck out of your house, went to a party you were not supposed to go to, or were drinking alcohol or abusing drugs. In most cases, authorities and parents will concentrate on the larger issues and be understanding about the minor ones.

Victims of incest or assault by an adult family friend, mentor, or foster parent may not report the crime because of the shame involved. Greg LeMond said in a 2009 *Los Angeles Times* interview, "The stigma is so bad that most people don't even want to talk about it. A lot of men won't even admit it."

Finally, some victims think that reporting the rape will not do any good and that most rape cases never go to trial. According to DOJ figures obtained by RAINN, 60 percent of rapes will never be reported. Only 10 percent of reports lead to an arrest. Only 4 percent lead to a felony conviction. Only 3 percent of convicted rapists will go to jail. Rape survivor Marianne Kirby, in the book *Dear Sister: Letters from Survivors of Sexual Violence*, writes about the difficult choice of whether to report the crime or not:

> To report a rape can mean being further victimized not just by the victim-blaming system

but also by the support structures we thought we had in place, like friends and family and school social circles. It can mean being called a liar, and it can mean being accused of ruining young men's lives. In some ways, it feels like a catch-22—if we don't report sexual assault, no one realizes how extensive the problem is and nothing changes; if we do report sexual assault, we are disbelieved and mocked and shamed and interrogated and blamed. And nothing changes.

But unless victims report the attack, rapists will still continue to think they can get away with their crimes.

There is another important reason for making a police report. During a rape, victims feel powerless to stop the assault. After the rape, they again feel powerless to protect themselves. Victims may feel better when they find ways to regain a sense of personal power and control. Making a report is one way to do something about what happened to them.

The police will ask you questions about what occurred before, during, and after the assault. They will go over all the details of your attack several times. They want to make sure your report is as detailed as possible to make a strong case against your rapist. You can have a family member or an advocate from the local rape crisis center with you during the questioning.

It is understandable that after a rape, victims want to go home, try to forget as much as possible of the event, and move on with their lives. They did not cause the rape, and they do not want to relive it numerous times for medical and police professionals. Survivors will tell you, however, that working to bring rapists to justice is an important step in recovery. You can't undo the rape. You can possibly prevent the rapist from thinking he can do it again.

PRESSING CHARGES

Rape victims are sometimes reluctant to press charges and build legal cases against their rapists. They must retell the stories of their rape to many different people, some of whom may not believe them. Law enforcement and legal representatives may ask intrusive questions about a victim's sexual history or how she was dressed. Survivors often call this situation a second rape. A rape crisis counselor or victim advocate is helpful during this stage.

A prosecutor usually makes the decision of what, if any,

Appearing in court as the victim of rape can be traumatic. Convicting a rapist may prevent another sexual assault, though, and put a rapist behind bars.

criminal charges to bring against an offender. Prosecutors want to win the case. If you decide to press charges, a prosecutor will want to know if there is enough credible evidence to convince a judge or jury that you were forcibly raped. The prosecutor will also want to make sure that if you are called to testify, you will be able to withstand intense questioning from the defense attorney. Sitting in a witness box, in front of a large group of strangers, telling again the intimate details of your assault can be traumatizing.

Prosecutors have other options besides taking the perpetrator to court. They can offer the rapist a plea deal. For example, in some states, first-degree criminal sexual conduct consists of forced penetration. This crime is punishable up to life imprisonment. Second-degree criminal sexual conduct consists of forced sexual contact, punishable by up to fifteen years imprisonment. Even though a case may involve forced penetration, the prosecutor may allow, or even encourage, the perpetrator to plead guilty to the lesser offense of second degree. This benefits the criminal justice system in that an expensive, possibly unwinnable trial is avoided. It benefits the victim in that he or she does not need to go through a trial. The rapist will be penalized and serve time in jail. However, the victim may feel as though her ordeal has not been treated seriously and the rapist did not get the sentence he deserved. Dr. Patti Feuereisen, author of the book *Invisible Girls: The Truth About Sexual Abuse*, gives this advice about taking the case to court:

You must never let anyone force you to report abuse. And the people around you should support your choice...If you decide that prosecuting is part of speaking your truth and healing, then use the criminal justice system well. Be prepared, have advocates, and know that no matter what happens in the courts, you have spoken your truth, and it was not your fault.

Very few rapists get convicted of their crime. There may be evidence that sexual intercourse occurred. But without injuries to the victim, prosecutors have a difficult time proving that the sex wasn't consensual.

Rape victims face numerous problems in the criminal justice system. They may not have the emotional or financial resources to spend long days in court or attorney's offices. They can become confused by why and how things happen in court. They can become intimidated by court proceedings, especially if it is their first time in the criminal justice system. They can also be intimidated by the defense attorney. Victims may find that many of the people involved in their case believe the myths about rape. These are some of the reasons why victims are grateful for the help they get from rape crisis centers.

RAPE CRISIS CENTERS

Just about every medium to large community, and many small communities, have a rape crisis center (RCC). These centers were organized during the feminist

Rape crisis center volunteers go through training so they can offer sexual assault victims information and support. Victims can expect that their conversations will be confidential.

movement in the 1960s and '70s. Staffed mainly by volunteers, the RCCs offered twenty-four-hour hotlines, legal and medical help, emotional support, counseling, and referrals to professionals. Antirape activists were successful in raising awareness about rape. They worked toward changes in laws, such as preventing a victim's sexual history from becoming admissible evidence and eliminating the requirement that the victim must have physically resisted the attack.

College students today will likely see notices for the nearest RCC on campus bulletin boards. These notices will list a phone number to call and the services offered. Middle and high school students may have a harder time finding a phone number to call. RAINN has responded with one central number that uses the area code from a caller to direct the call to the nearest RCC. An Internet search for "rape crisis center" will direct you to local centers. Calling 911 about a rape will connect

Posters and brochures advertising rape crisis centers are often found on college bulletin boards. Most of the services offered by these centers are free or low cost.

you to police. If the situation is not dangerous, a call to your phone carrier's 411 number can connect you with the nearest crisis call center.

A rape crisis center is a public organization that has no other role than providing emotional support to victims. Doctors are mainly concerned with injuries, police officers are concerned with collecting evidence, and prosecutors are building a case. The RCC helps victims sort out these sometimes competing interests.

A community's rape crisis center is more than just a resource to victims. It provides valuable assistance to other community agencies. It provides education and training to those on the front lines of sexual assault: law enforcement, hospital staff, local and state

Girls can empower themselves by learning effective self-defense techniques. Classes in self-defense are offered by rape crisis centers, YWCAs, and community recreation agencies.

lawmakers, and the criminal justice system. It may offer classes in rape prevention and self-defense.

A volunteer usually answers the phone at an RCC, as the centers do not have budgets for a lot of paid positions. The volunteer is trained to offer calm advice about the various options available to a rape victim and how to access the center's resources. The volunteer is often a survivor as well. If you call an RCC, you do not have to give any identifying information to get your questions answered. You may want to take advantage of the services offered. For instance, you may want a legal or medical advocate to accompany you to the police station or hospital. The advocates may provide you with the pros and cons of making a police report or deciding to prosecute. They probably will not influence you one way or another. These are your decisions to make.

Rape crisis centers throughout the United States and Canada receive hundreds of thousands of calls each day.

RAINN

The Rape, Abuse & Incest National Network (RAINN) is the largest anti–sexual violence organization in the United States. RAINN created and operates the National Sexual Assault Hotline (800-656-HOPE [4673]), directing calls to the main number to a caller's local rape crisis center. It also provides services and information on its website at www.rainn.org. In addition to offering confidential advice to rape victims, it offers programs to prevent sexual violence and to help ensure that rapists are brought to justice.

Yet not many rape victims take advantage of the services offered. The 2007 Rape in Utah Survey shows that only 3 percent of rape victims contacted a rape crisis line. Teens are especially concerned that no one find out about the rape. Even though they realize the rape was not their fault, they worry that others will judge them or hold them responsible.

FINDING HELP ONLINE

Some sexual assault victims may not want to talk to a rape crisis counselor or may not have access to a private phone. Many rape crisis centers offer an online hotline with a chat feature. For instance, RAINN has a twenty-four-hour online chat hotline staffed with trained counselors. It is secure and completely confidential. The counselors can refer victims to resources in their local areas that can meet their needs.

No one wants to become the victim of a horrible crime and become involved in the criminal justice system. No one should have to. Yet rapes happen and teens are forced to deal with the aftermath. Rape victims who allow family and friends, doctors and nurses, and victims' advocates and counselors to help them become survivors. Teen rape survivors with support are able to help police and prosecutors bring rapists to justice. It is never easy. Sexual assault survivors play a key role in preventing perpetrators from commiting future assaults. This process doesn't compensate for the rape. It can, however, bring peace to the survivor.

CHAPTER 5

After Neesha Arter's rape, her parents pressed charges. However, the prosecutor in the case decided there wasn't enough evidence to go to trial. Neesha looked for some sense of control during the legal battle. The only control she could find was in what she ate. She writes in her *Teen Vogue* article:

> I became consumed by an obsession with calories, an obsession with making myself disappear. My friends never knew I had been to a rape clinic or that I had spoken with detectives. I was too ashamed to tell anyone, so I began to isolate myself. I spent the year in solitude with these disturbing memories. I lost my trust in everyone and lived in fear. For the rest of high school, I chose to push away the trauma, but I woke up years later still broken.

Neesha's experience is not uncommon for rape survivors. Many relive the trauma every night in nightmares. Other survivors begin cutting themselves, gain a lot of weight, or become promiscuous. The ways of coping, whether in a healthy way or in a destructive way, are as varied as the survivors who use them. After several years of therapy, Neesha regained her health.

After a sexual assault, victims often find it difficult to cope with their intense feelings. Accepting help is an important step toward recovery.

She says, "I had to face the darkness so it could set me free." There are several names for the ordeal Neesha went through after her assault. Some therapists call it rape trauma syndrome. Others use the more general term post-traumatic stress disorder (PTSD). Whatever one calls it, the process of working through the aftermath of rape can be difficult, almost overwhelming. Most victims say they couldn't have survived it without help.

THE ACUTE PHASE OF RECOVERY

For most survivors, the period right after a sexual assault is one of confusing and conflicting emotions. Some victims tell themselves that they are fine, and they are grateful that they still have their lives to live. Inside, however, they feel guilt that they somehow caused the rape, fear that the rapist will return, sadness that they lost their innocence, and doubt that they will ever forget the horrifying details. RAINN calls this period the acute phase. It tends to last a few days to several weeks.

Sasha Walters was thirteen when she was raped by a sixteen-year-old boy at a summer resort. In *Dear Sister*, she says, "I lost my childhood. I lost my innocence, I learned that rapists take what they want, even if they look like—or literally are—the boy next door." She, like many survivors, felt disoriented and had difficulty concentrating and making decisions. Though victims may look fine, inside they are still in shock that the event occurred.

THE OUTWARD ADJUSTMENT PHASE

After a few weeks, rape survivors are expected to resume normal life. They enter the outward adjustment phase. They use various coping techniques to get through their days. Some victims pretend that everything is fine and that they have recovered. They may refuse to talk about the assault. Others do the opposite. They cannot stop talking about the rape and cannot forget the details. Another coping technique is to move away from the social circle in which the rape occurred. Some survivors insist on changing schools and changing their group of friends. They cut or color their hair and change their style of clothes in an attempt to escape the pain.

It is during this period that dysfunctional behaviors may appear. Adrienne Maree Brown, another victim who includes a letter in *Dear Sister,* describes her reactions to her rape. "First, I gained weight. Looking back, I think I didn't want anyone looking at me. At the time I wasn't aware of it, but I just suddenly felt a dependency and longing for the comfort of chocolate, pizza, bread." Eating and sleeping difficulties are common in this phase. Some victims lose their ability to feel deeply. Letter writer Renee Martin describes it this way: "The numbness sets in and rather than dealing with the rage and the pain, you think that it is better not to feel anything at all." Sasha Walters began acting out in destructive ways. She

Rape victims may lose interest in such everyday activities as eating, exercising, and socializing with friends.

says, "After I was raped, I became withdrawn and then promiscuous, and I gravitated to abusive boys. I really lost my will to say no."

Dr. Patti Feuereisen, who collected rape survivor stories in her book *Invisible Girls*, wrote the story of Dahlia, who developed an eating disorder after her ordeal:

> I felt out of control. Now running track was not enough. I needed to control something else, and about the only other thing I could control was my eating...My little world at the time revolved around eating and purging, around counting calories and checking for pinchable flesh. I was determined never to have any flesh that could be pinched. I figured that if I didn't look like a woman, if I had no curves, no breasts, no flesh, maybe I wouldn't be rape-able, maybe I wouldn't be sexual. Maybe I would disappear.

Anxiety, mood swings, and fears and phobias are all things that may plague rape survivors. The attack may negatively impact their relationships with current boyfriends or girlfriends. Their academic and athletic performance may suffer. They lose motivation to do anything, including help themselves recover. Just when they need their friends and family the most, they may withdraw from the people they love and who love them. RAINN reports that victims of sexual assault are three times more likely to suffer from depression than non-victims, thirteen times more likely to abuse alcohol,

Depression and anxiety after a sexual assault may push teens into self-destructive behaviors, such as smoking, drinking alcohol, or abusing drugs.

twenty-six times more likely to abuse drugs, and four times more likely to consider suicide. These negative consequences of experiencing a sexual assault can last for years. Greg LeMond says, "The shame is so great that it ends up eating you up inside. You end up being self-destructive or depressed. The key is to get past the shame and live a life that's not shame-driven."

Male victims of rape feel similar emotions to female victims. They may also feel as if the attack made them "less of a man." Gay teens may feel that the crime is a "punishment" for their sexual orientation. They may feel targeted because they were gay. Heterosexual teens may fear that others will perceive them as gay. Rape counselors reassure victims that a rape cannot change one's sexual orientation, nor is it any kind of statement about a person's masculinity.

CYBERBULLYING AND VICTIM RECOVERY

One reason why rape victims are reluctant to press charges against their attackers is the fear that they will be blamed for the crime. Some recent high-profile sexual assaults of teens by their peers that blew up in the media show that the fear is real. Just when victims should be concentrating their energies on recovery, they find themselves bullied on social media sites with vicious attacks on their behavior and character. The victim in the Steubenville gang rape received death threats.

A private tragedy such as sexual assault can become public when spread through social media. Rape victims become targets of bullying on Facebook, Twitter, and other social media platforms.

Another high-profile case revealed the role the media plays in public bullying of rape victims. In 2013, two star football players in Torrington, Connecticut, were arrested for sexually assaulting two thirteen-year-old girls. Students and citizens took the debate over the guilt of the young men to social media, using graphic and vulgar language and photographs. According to a 2013 *Connecticut Magazine* article, one student called the girls "snitch" and accused them of "ruining the lives" of the athletes. Another wrote on Twitter, "Even if it was all his fault, what was a 13 year old girl doing hanging around 18 year old guys." Yet another wrote, "If it takes two then why is only one in trouble?" The young men eventually pleaded guilty to second-degree sexual assault and received jail sentences.

Several sexual assault victims were so harassed

by their peers that they ended their lives by suicide. Rehtaeh Parsons was fifteen when she was sexually assaulted by four boys in Nova Scotia, Canada, in 2013. Photos of the rape circulated among her peers, and the cyberbullying became intense. She attempted to kill herself by hanging but ended up in a coma. She was eventually taken off life support and allowed to die. Like Audrie Pott, she could not endure the hell her life had become. The case prompted Canada to pass a cyberbullying law.

These cases are extreme. Very few rape victims take their own lives. In fact, most recover and go on to live happy, productive lives. And most of these men and women attribute their recovery to professional therapy and the love, support, and understanding of friends and family. *Dear Sister* letter writer River Willow Fagan expresses her message of hope to other survivors:

> Perhaps, like me, you sometimes feel like everything inside of you is broken, like the pain has cut you so deeply that it defines you, like he or she or they scooped out everything beautiful and fine and strong within you and filled you up instead with burning bile, corrosive poison, endless shame...But there is another voice within me, gentle and strong, and it says, there is a place inside of you that the violence never touched, a place inside of you where no violence can ever touch.

If you have a friend who has been sexually assaulted, you want to provide understanding and support. Below are some tips.

- Let your friend know that you will support any decision he or she makes about reporting the crime or not.
- Do not blame or judge by asking "why" questions.
- Do not ask for details. The survivor may find the assault humiliating to talk about.
- Do not force the victim to take actions before he or she is ready.
- Be a good listener.
- Resist the urge to seek revenge against the person who committed the assault.
- Reassure the survivor that your friendship and support has not changed because of the rape.
- Don't be angry if a friend did not immediately disclose the assault. Survivors need to move at their own speed.

How to Help a Friend Who Has Been Raped

FINDING A THERAPIST

Most experts on trauma, especially the trauma associated with sexual assault, say that professional therapy can be the single biggest aid to recovery. RAINN says

that getting treatment as soon as possible can prevent long-term problems with depression, anxiety, or PTSD. However, according to the 2007 Utah survey, only 38 percent of rape victims talked to a rape counselor. Most waited more than a year to make the first appointment. Only 10 percent sought help within the first week.

There are many reasons why rape survivors don't seek therapy as part of the recovery process. They may think they don't need counseling and that they can recover on their own. They may not know how to find counseling services in their communities. They may not have told their families and

A mental health professional can help sexual assault victims work through their feelings of fear, anxiety, and anger. Friends and family who listen can also help with recovery.

don't have the resources to access counseling on their own. They may think their families cannot afford counseling.

Victims do not have to let any of these reasons become barriers to getting therapy after a rape. Their nearest rape crisis center can provide referrals to low- or no-cost counseling. This may include private counseling, where victims can process the assault with a trained therapist. Some victims may prefer to meet in a group setting with others who have had similar experiences. Groups have been proved effective in offering support to victims who may feel isolated because of their trauma.

Group therapy and support groups have been proven to be very effective for survivors of rape and sexual abuse. Talking with other survivors who understand your experience can help you feel less isolated.

If you do decide to follow up on referrals to a therapist, how do you know how to choose one? One way to decide if a therapist is right for you is to pay attention to how you feel around him or her. Do you feel heard when you speak? Does the therapist put you at ease? Does he or she help you understand your feelings? Does he or she provide practical steps for resuming normal life? Not every victim finds the right therapist with the first phone call. It is OK to decide one isn't working for you and try another.

Survivors of rape may think they will never recover. They may worry that they will live with the nightmares, anxiety, and fear for the rest of their lives. Survivors who allow friends and family to support them will find that their panic attacks subside and their sleep becomes peaceful again. Those survivors who seek therapy for more serious symptoms such as self-harm, eating disorders, or substance abuse will also find that they can overcome these behaviors. The sexual assault becomes part of their past that need not continually intrude on the present.

1. What are the danger signs that a date may turn into rape?

2. My girlfriend and I want to have sex. Can I be arrested for rape?

3. I'm gay, and my boyfriend assaulted me. I am not ready to come out yet. Where can I go for help?

4. How can DNA be used to identify a rapist?

5. I am scared to walk to my car after work at night. How can I protect myself?

6. Do boys who have been sexually abused as children always become abusers themselves?

7. Why are date rape cases hard to prove?

8. What if I want to report my rape several months after it happened?

9. Can I get a medical exam or counseling without my parents' knowledge or consent?

10. If I report the rape to the police, will they tell my parents?

10 GREAT QUESTIONS TO ASK A THERAPIST, MEDICAL PROFESSIONAL, OR LAW ENFORCEMENT PROFESSIONAL

Because of the publicity of the White House Task Force to Protect Students from Sexual Assault in 2014, college campuses have upgraded campus lighting and parking lot emergency call boxes. These steps are important. However, according to the U.S. Bureau of Justice Statistics, only 8 percent of rapes of college women are by unknown men jumping out from behind parked cars or dark buildings.

When many people think of rape prevention, they think of self-defense classes and well-lit sidewalks. What they need to think of, according to rape experts, are ways to educate themselves on the reality of rape, its connection to binge drinking, and the meaning of consent. Teens need to learn who is at risk for becoming a victim or perpetrator of rape and how their beliefs may contribute to sexual violence. As they head into the dating world, teens need to learn about enforcing personal boundaries and practice nonviolent conflict resolution skills.

THE PERPETRATORS AND VICTIMS OF RAPE

Law enforcement personnel and rape researchers agree that there is no one rapist profile. Rapists are a heterogeneous population, which

Rapists come in different colors, ages, and sizes, but many men who engage in sexual assault share certain characteristics. They can be impulsive, heavy drinkers, and hostile toward women.

means that there are all kinds of sex offenders. However, the Sexual Assault Prevention and Awareness Center (SAPAC) of the University of Michigan put together a list of characteristics. Though these apply to young men between the ages of eighteen and twenty-two, they can generalize to younger teen boys as well (and 99 percent of perpetrators in this age group are male).

SAPAC researchers found that young men who commit sexual assault are more likely to believe traditional stereotypes about gender roles. For instance, they believe that men are responsible for initiating sex and women are responsible for setting limits. They often justify the rape with statements such as "girls say no when they mean yes" and "girls like forced sex."

Other personality characteristics of men who commit sexual assault are lack of empathy, hostility toward women, and dominant and controlling personalities. They were less concerned about the effect of their behavior on other people. They were impulsive and consumed alcohol at a higher rate than most young men. They were more likely to be involved with communities where their actions were likely to go unpunished, such as on sports teams or in college fraternities.

On a date, young men who went on to sexually assault the girls they were with tended to insist on being alone with her. They displayed anger or aggression against the victim and often acted jealous or possessive. They ignored the victim's wishes and attempted to make her feel guilty about not giving in to them. They became more hostile and aggressive when she said no.

Entrepreneurs have created some innovative tools to help teens and young adults avoid becoming victims of rape. Circle of 6 is a smartphone app that allows users to choose six friends to contact easily if they are in a situation in which they need help. The app uses GPS to find nearby friends who can provide an interruption or a ride home. SPOT a Problem is an app that works with a wristband that a party host wears. The wristband lights up when a party guest sends an alert that someone might be in trouble. Undercover Colors, developed by students at North Carolina State University, is a nail polish that detects date rape drugs when the wearer dips her finger in a drink containing them.

Avoiding a date rape has become easier with innovative tools such as phone apps that connect nearby friends and a nail polish that detects date rape drugs in drinks.

There is less research on victims than on perpetrators. Victims of sexual assault tend to be less assertive than most women and have lower self-esteem.

THE RESPONSIBILITY OF BYSTANDERS

For several hours outside a 2009 homecoming dance at a Richmond, California, high school, twenty people watched while a fifteen-year-old girl was gang-raped and beaten. Some took pictures. Others laughed. Like the rape in Steubenville, no one stepped in to stop the assault. Finally, an eighteen-year-old woman called the police. According to an *East Bay News* story, one of the bystanders said, "I feel like I could have done something but I don't feel like I have any responsibility for anything that happened." What can be done to engage bystanders to stop the sexual violence they witness? Quite a lot, says Jennifer Benner, a specialist with the National Sexual Violence Resource Center (NSVRC), on the organization's website.

Benner reminds everyone, "As a community member, you play a critical role in preventing these crimes by showing through your words and actions that relationships must be based on respect, equality, safety, and consent." She tells her readers to speak up when they hear jokes about rape and call out inappropriate behavior. At a party, she advises teens to be responsible for making sure that friends get home safely. She asks that teens and young adults challenge violent and abusive comments on social media.

Bystanders who witness a sexual assault can potentially prevent a tragedy by calling the police.

NSVRC is one of many organizations that offer bystander education prevention programs. For instance, Mentors in Violence Prevention (MVP) involves student leaders and athletes in educating high school students about men's roles in gender violence prevention. The Men Can Stop Rape organization shows men how to take a stand against other men who harass or abuse women.

EDUCATING YOUR SCHOOL AND COMMUNITY

Teens can be extremely effective agents of change to affect their schools' tolerance for sexualized bullying. Students can take the lead in bringing educational programs to their school. For instance, the Rape Recovery Center in Utah offers programs for middle school through college. The program Boundary, Limits & Communication gets middle school students talking about appropriate and inappropriate relationship behaviors. The high school program targets male students in discussions of sexist attitudes. One goal of the program is to help students learn about nonviolent conflict resolution skills and how they can be used in real-life dating situations.

There are many organizations that high school students can bring to their campus. Men Can Stop Rape offers help in setting up a Men of Strength (MOST) Club. This organization offers middle and high school boys a supportive space to learn about healthy masculinity. White Ribbon is an organization that started in Canada in 1991 to provide education for young men and women in ways to prevent sexual violence. Its Make the Call targets high school student athletes to address gender-based violence in schools. Love Is Respect is an organization dedicated to fostering healthy dating among teens. It offers wallet cards, print materials, videos, and a website to teach teens about dating abuse.

TIPS FOR PERSONAL SAFETY

Though there is no way for teens—or anyone—to completely protect themselves from sexual assault, there are some practical safety tips that can help keep teens safe. Here are some tips for preventing the most common type of teen assault: acquaintance rape.

At parties:
- Go with a group of friends and check in with each other often. They can help you get out of a bad situation. Take it upon yourself to help get friends out of bad situations. Have each other's backs.
- Trust your instincts. If your gut is telling you someone is dangerous, get away.
- Don't drink alcohol. For any drink, including soft drinks, don't leave it unattended. Don't take drinks out of a punchbowl. Don't accept a

drink from someone else. If you have left your drink while in the restroom, get another one.

On a date:

- If you don't know your date well, plan for social settings, such as going to a movie, bowling, or a sports event.

- Be true to yourself. Your date should accept "because I don't want to" as a reason to refuse anything, such as an alcoholic drink, a touch, or an intimate situation. If he doesn't, tell him you want to leave.

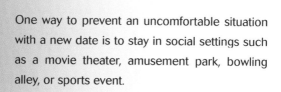

One way to prevent an uncomfortable situation with a new date is to stay in social settings such as a movie theater, amusement park, bowling alley, or sports event.

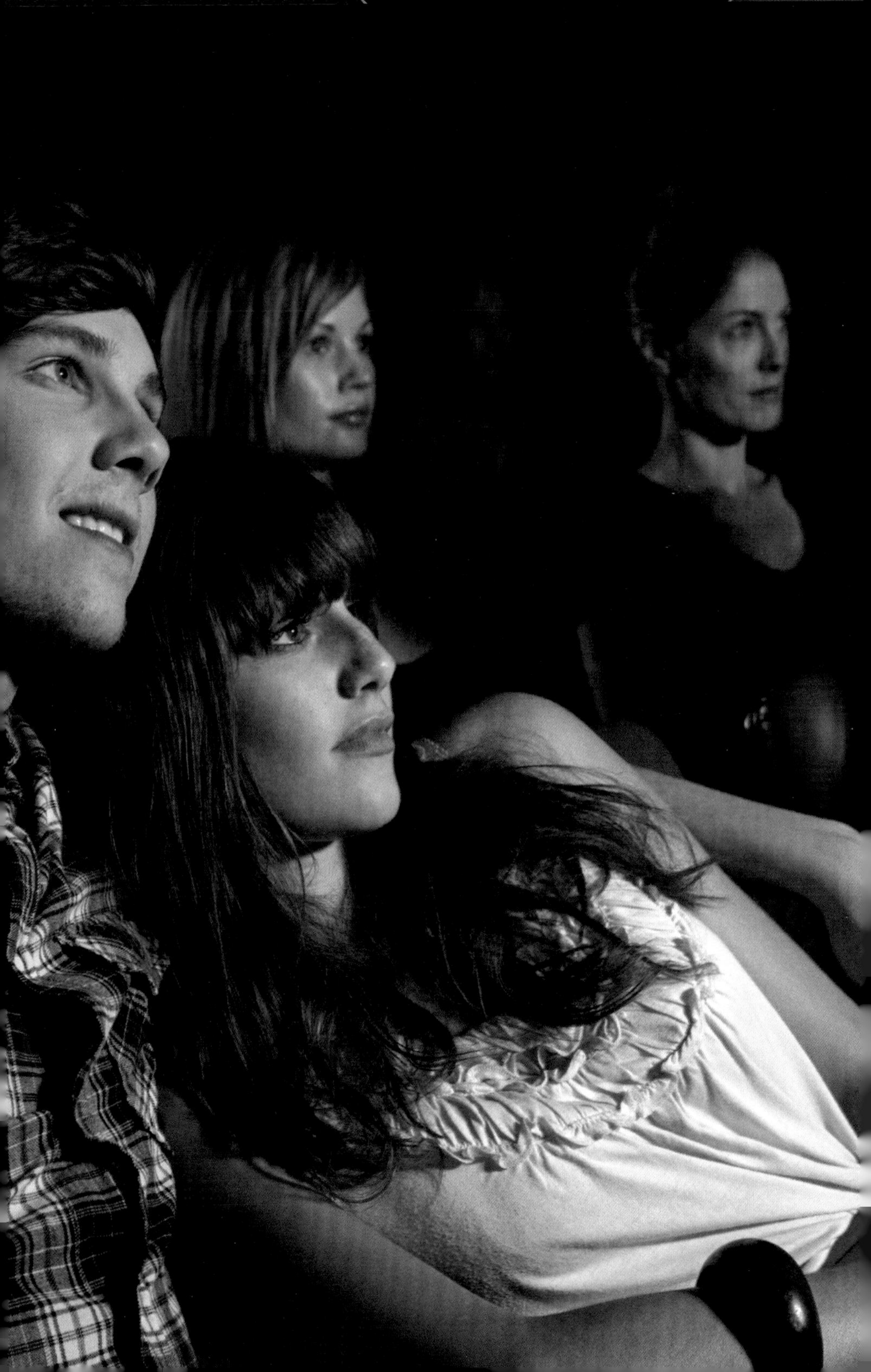

- Have a code word with friends or family. If you don't feel comfortable, you can call them, and they can come get you.
- Be honest. Tell your date you need more time to get to know him or her before continuing with intimacy.
- Be prepared to lie if you need to get out of an uncomfortable situation. Tell your date you don't feel well, or you are concerned about someone at home.
- Be alert for escape routes. Are there people around who might help you?
- Always carry enough money for a cab home and have a cab company phone number in your phone contacts list.

As a bystander:
- If you witness an assault, call 911 immediately. While giving your name is best, being anonymous is better than not calling at all.
- If it is safe, step in and offer assistance. Don't leave if you don't have to. A perpetrator is less likely to do something in front of a witness.

How can you prevent stranger rape?
- Don't go anywhere by yourself, especially if you are unsure of the area.

Friendships that begin with a foundation of respect can develop into mature romantic relationships.

- Always be aware of your surroundings. Walking with headphones on will make it hard to hear someone coming up behind you.

Sexual assaults are less likely to happen to teens who walk confidently, are aware of their surroundings, and avoid dangerous areas.

- Avoid isolated areas. There may be no one around to answer a call for help.
- Walk quickly, as if you know exactly where you are going and need to get there quickly.
- Go with your instincts. If a place or situation feels unsafe, leave.
- Always carry a charged cell phone and enough money to get a cab home.

You do not need to live in constant fear that you will be raped. Statistics show, however, that sexual assault may touch your life at some point. You may have a friend or family member who is raped. It may happen to you. If so, it will affect every aspect of your life and change you forever. You will be a different person, a stronger person, as a result of your experience. Despite the assault, you can have a wonderful, fulfilling life.

By taking advantage of the resources available to you, as well as the support of those who love you, you can become a survivor. You can forgive yourself, lose the guilt, and move forward courageously. You cannot change what happened to you. You can choose not to let it define your life.

GLOSSARY

advocate A person who publicly supports a cause or policy.

anonymous Not identified by name.

consensual Relating to or involving consent, especially mutual consent.

constitute To be the same as or form something.

convicted Found guilty of a crime.

custodial rape Assault of a child by a non-family member who has custody of the child.

cutting A form of self-injury in which someone cuts himself or herself to cope with emotional pain.

cyberbullying The use of information technology to repeatedly harm or harass other people in a deliberate manner.

derogatory Expressing a low opinion of someone or something.

dysfunctional Not operating normally.

emergency contraception pills (ECPs) Medicine taken after unprotected sexual intercourse to prevent pregnancy.

forensic Using scientific methods and techniques to investigate a crime.

fraternity A social organization for college men.

gang rape Rape by a group of people.

heterogeneous Made up of a diverse mixture.

incapacitated Unable to work or function in the correct way.

incest Sexual activity between family members or close relatives.

inhibition A feeling that makes one unable to act in a relaxed and natural way.

inordinate Unusually large, or excessive.

intoxicated State of losing control of behavior and actions due to the influence of drugs or alcohol.

"liquid courage" Slang term for the effects alcohol can have in terms of lowering inhibitions.

mandatory Required by law.

mentor rape Sexual assault by a trusted adviser against the person he or she is mentoring.

misogynistic Showing a dislike or mistrust of women.

offender Person who commits an illegal act or crime.

orifice An opening in the body, such as a nostril or anus.

perpetrator Person who has committed a crime.

post-traumatic stress disorder (PTSD) Anxiety disorder that results from experiencing trauma.

prison rape Rape of a prison inmate by a prison guard or fellow inmate.

promiscuous Having casual sex frequently with different partners.

prophylaxis Measures designed to preserve health and prevent disease.

prosecution The institution that conducts legal proceedings against a person accused of a crime.

rape Penetration of an orifice by another person without consent.

rape culture Concept that our society's attitudes about gender and sexuality allow for rape to be wide-spread and acceptable.

rape kit Evidence collected after a rape or sexual assault.

sedatives A category of drugs that slow normal brain function.

sexual assault Involuntary sexual act.

sexual intercourse Sexual contact between individuals that involves penetration.

spousal rape The act of a spouse forcing sex on the other without his or her consent.

statutory Referring to a law enacted by a state, city, or county.

stereotype Commonly held, oversimplified beliefs about a person or group of people that may or may not be true.

token resistance The false idea that when people on dates say no, they really mean yes and their protests are not to be taken seriously.

toxicology The science dealing with the effects of poisonous substances in the body.

trauma A physical injury or emotionally disturbing experience.

vulnerable Open to attack.

war rape The use of rape as a war tactic. Rape used as a weapon to terrorize individual women and girls, their families, and entire communities.

FOR MORE INFORMATION

Advocates for Youth
2000 M Street NW, Suite 750
Washington, DC 20036
(202) 419-3420
Website: http://www.advocatesforyouth.org

Advocates for Youth supports efforts that help young people make informed and responsible decisions about their reproductive and sexual health. It advocates for a positive and realistic approach to adolescent sexual health.

Break the Cycle
6029 Bristol Parkway, Suite 201
Culver City, CA 90230
(310) 286-3383
Website: http://www.breakthecycle.org

Break the Cycle is a nonprofit organization working to provide dating abuse prevention programs to youth. Its mission is to inspire and support young people to build healthy relationships and create a culture without abuse.

Love Is Respect
P.O. Box 16180
Austin, TX 78716
(866) 331-9474
Website: http://www.loveisrespect.org

Love Is Respect is a project of the National Domestic Violence Hotline and Break the Cycle. This organization provides resources to engage, educate, and empower youth and young adults to prevent and end abusive relationships.

Men Can Stop Rape
1130 6th Street NW, Suite 100
Washington, DC 20001
(202) 265-6530
Website: http://www.mencanstoprape.org

Men Can Stop Rape is an international organization that gets youth involved in ending men's violence against women. It teaches men to use their strength to help create a world of peace, understanding, and equality between the sexes.

1in6, Inc.
P.O. Box 222033
Santa Clarita, CA 91322
Website: https://1in6.org

This organization helps men who have had unwanted or abusive sexual experiences in childhood live healthier, happier lives.

Rape, Abuse & Incest National Network (RAINN)
1220 L Street NW, Suite 505
Washington, DC 20005
(202) 544-1034
Website: https://www.rainn.org

RAINN is the United States' largest anti–sexual violence organization. It operates the National Sexual Assault Hotline and provides victims of sexual assault with free, confidential services. It also carries out programs to prevent sexual violence, help victims, and ensure that rapists are brought to justice.

White Ribbon Campaign
365 Bloor Street East, Suite 203
Toronto, ON M4W 3L4
Canada
(416) 920-6684
Website: http://www.whiteribbon.ca

White Ribbon is the world's largest movement of men and boys working to end violence against women and girls and promote gender equality, healthy relationships, and a new vision of masculinity.

WEBSITES

Because of the changing nature of Internet links, Rosen Publishing has developed an online list of websites related to the subject of this book. This site is updated regularly. Please use this link to access the list:

Http://www.rosenlinks.com/411/Raped

FOR FURTHER READING

Anderson, Laurie Halse. *Speak*. New York, NY: Puffin, 2001.

Arterburn, Stephen, Fred Stoeker, and Mike Yorkey. *Preparing Your Son for Every Man's Battle: Honest Conversations About Sexual Integrity*. Colorado Springs, CO: WaterBrook Press, 2010.

Blow, Charles. *Fire Shut Up in My Bones*. New York, NY: Houghton Mifflin Harcourt, 2014.

Bourke, Joanna. *Sex, Violence, History*. Berkeley, CA: Shoemaker Hoard, 2007.

Bryant-Davis, Thema, ed. *Surviving Sexual Violence: A Guide to Recovery and Empowerment*. Lanham, MD: Rowman & Littlefield, 2011.

Eastham, Chad. *The Truth About Dating, Love, and Just Being Friends*. Nashville, TN: Thomas Nelson Inc., 2011.

Fonda, Jane. *Being a Teen: Everything Teen Girls & Boys Should Know About Relationships, Sex, Love, Health, Identity & More*. New York, NY: Random House, 2014.

Gerdes, Louise I. *Teen Dating* (Opposing Viewpoints Series). Farmington Hills, MI: Greenhaven Press, 2013.

Henderson, Elisabeth, and Nancy Armstrong. *100 Questions You'd Never Ask Your Parents: Straight Answers to Teen Questions About Sex,*

Sexuality, and Health. New York, NY: Roaring Brook Press, 2013.

Hiber, Amanda, ed. *Sexual Violence* (Opposing Viewpoints Series). Farmington Hills, MI: Greenhaven Press, 2014.

Kehner, George. *Date Rape Drugs* (Drugs: The Straight Facts). Philadelphia, PA: Chelsea House Publishers, 2004.

Landau, Elaine. *Date Violence*. New York, NY: Franklin Watts, 2004.

Levy, Barrie. *In Love and in Danger: A Teen's Guide to Breaking Free of Abusive Relationships*. New York, NY: Seal Press, 2006.

Lily, Henrietta. *Dating Violence* (Teen Mental Health). New York, NY: Rosen Publishing Group, 2011.

Lohmann, Raychelle, and Julia Taylor. *The Bullying Workbook for Teens*. Oakland, CA: Instant Help Books, 2013.

McKinnon, Marjorie. *REPAIR for Teens: A Program for Recovery from Incest & Childhood Sexual Abuse*. Ann Arbor, MI: Loving Healing Press, 2012.

Meier, Katie. *A Girl's Guide to Life: The Truth on Growing Up, Being True, and Making Your Teen Years Fabulous*. Nashville, TN: Thomas Nelson Inc., 2010.

Palmer, Libbi. *The PTSD Workbook for Teens: Simple, Effective Skills for Healing Trauma*. Oakland, CA: Instant Help Books, 2012.

Pardes, Bronwen. *Doing It Right: Making Smart, Safe, and Satisfying Choices About Sex.* New York, NY: Simon Pulse, 2007.

Ream, Anne K. *Lived Through This: Listening to the Stories of Sexual Violence Survivors.* Boston, MA: Beacon Press, 2014.

Sebold, Alice. *Lucky: A Memoir.* New York, NY: Back Bay Books, 2002.

Stephens, Aarti D., ed. *Sexual Violence* (Opposing Viewpoints Series). Farmington Hills, MI: Greenhaven Press, 2012.

Waldal, Elin Stebbins. *Tornado Warning: A Memoir of Teen Dating Violence and Its Effect on a Woman's Life.* Encinitas, CA: Sound Beach, 2011.

Watkins, Christine, ed. *Date Rape* (At Issue). Farmington Hills, MI: Greenhaven Press, 2007.

Weisz, Arlene M., and Beverly M. Black. *Programs to Reduce Teen Dating Violence and Sexual Assault: Perspectives on What Works.* New York, NY: Columbia University Press, 2009.

Wilkins, Jessica. *Straight Talk About Date Rape* (Straight Talk About...). New York, NY: Crabtree Publishing Company, 2011.

BIBLIOGRAPHY

Abbey, Antonia, Tina Zawacki, Philip O. Buck, A. Monique Clinton, and Pam McAuslan. "Alcohol and Sexual Assault." National Institute on Alcohol Abuse and Alcoholism. Retrieved September 19, 2014 (http://pubs.niaaa.nih.gov/publications /arh25-1/43-51.htm).

Arter, Neesha. "Teenage Sexual Assault: One Girl's Eye-Opening Story." *Teen Vogue,* 2014. Retrieved September 9, 2014 (http://www.teenvogue.com/my -life/2013-11/teen-sexual-assault).

Benner, Jennifer. "Beyond Steubenville: Tools for Engaged Bystanders." March 15, 2013. National Sexual Violence Resource Center. Retrieved September 17, 2014 (http://www.nsvrc.org/blogs /preventionista/beyond-steubenville-tools-engaged -bystanders).

Burleigh, Nina. "Sexting, Shame and Suicide." *Rolling Stone,* September 17, 2013. Retrieved September 2014 (http://www.rollingstone.com/culture/news/sexting -shame-and-suicide-20130917).

Centers for Disease Control and Prevention. "The National Intimate Partner and Sexual Violence Survey." Retrieved July 28, 2014 (http://www.cdc.gov /violenceprevention/nisvs/index.html).

Crowe, Jerry. "One Phone Call Changed Greg LeMond's Life." *Los Angeles Times,* August 18, 2009. Retieved September 17, 2014 (http://articles.latimes.com/2009/ aug/18/sports/sp-crowe18).

Dean, Mensah. "Teen Gets 6 to 12 Years for Drunken Rape, Death." *Philadelphia Daily News*, July 29, 2010. Retrieved September 14, 2014 (http:articles.philly.com /2010-07-29/news/24972163_1_hard-liquor-juan -williams-hard-time).

Derienzo, Matt. "Rape Culture: Torrington, Connecticut, Confronts 'Blame the Victim' Mentality." *Connecticut Magazine*, May 2013. Retrieved September 10, 2014 (http://www .connecticutmag.com/Connecticut-Magazine/ May-2013/Rape-Culture).

Factora-Borchers, Lisa, ed. *Dear Sister: Letters from Survivors of Sexual Violence*. Oakland, CA: AK Press, 2014.

Feuereisen, Patti. *Invisible Girls: The Truth About Sexual Abuse*. Emeryville, CA: Seal Press, 2009.

Hiber, Amanda, ed. *Sexual Violence* (Opposing Viewpoints Series). Farmington Hills, MI: Greenhaven Press, 2014.

Huffingtonpost.com. "Roast Busters, New Zealand 'Teen Rape Club,' Allegedly Preyed On Drunk, Underage Girls." November 6, 2013. Retrieved September 17, 2014 (http://www.huffingtonpost.com/2013/11/06 /roast-busters-new-zealand-teen-rape-club_n _4221597.html).

Kehner, George. *Date Rape Drugs* (Drugs: The Straight Facts). Philadelphia, PA: Chelsea House Publishers, 2004.

Mitchell, Christine, and Benjamin Peterson. "Rape in Utah 2007." Utah Commission on Criminal and Juvenile Justice, 2007. Retrieved July 28, 2014 (http://www.justice.utah.gov/Documents/Research /SexOffender/RapeinUtah2007.pdf).

Murguia, Stephany. "Wasatch High Officials' 'Modesty Shaming' of Female Students Is Outrageous." Rape Recovery Center Blog, May 29, 2014. Retrieved September 15, 2014 (https://raperecoverycenter.org /news/wasatch-high-officials-modesty-shaming-of -female-students-is-outrageous).

North Carolina Coalition Against Sexual Assault. "Summary of North Carolina Sex Crimes as of March 2011." Retrieved September 25, 2014 (http://www .nccasa.org/cms/wp-content/uploads/2014/01 /SUMMARY-OF-NORTH-CAROLINA-SEX -CRIMES-as-of-March-2011-1.pdf).

Oppal, Richard. "Ohio Teenagers Guilty in Rape That Social Media Brought to Light." *New York Times*, March 17, 2013. Retrieved July 28, 2014 (http://www .nytimes.com/2013/03/18/us/ teenagers-found-guilty-in-rape-in-steubenville -ohio.html?pagewanted=all).

Perry, David. "Rape Cases: When Judges Just Don't Get It." CNN Opinion, May 5, 2014. Retrieved September 8, 2014 (http://www.cnn.com/2014/03/11/opinion /perry-rape-disabled-georgia).

Rape, Abuse & Incest National Network. "Reporting Rates." 2009. Retrieved September 25, 2014 (https://www.rainn.org/get-information/statistics /reporting-rates).

Sexual Assault Prevention & Awareness Center. "Understanding the Perpetrator." Retrieved September 25, 2014 (http://sapac.umich.edu/article/196).

United Nations News Centre. "UNICEF Adviser Says Rape in Darfur, Sudan Continues with Impunity." October, 19, 2004. Retrieved September 16, 2014 (http://www.un.org/apps/news/story.asp?NewsID= 12280&Cr=darfur&Cr1=).

United States Commission on Civil Rights. "Sexual Assault in the Military." September 2013. Retrieved September 16, 2014 (http://www.usccr.gov/pubs/ 09242013_Statutory_Enforcement_Report_Sexual _Assault_in_the_Military.pdf).

United States Department of Justice. "Attorney General Eric Holder Announces Revisions to the Uniform Crime Report's Definition of Rape." January 6, 2012. Retrieved September 25, 2014 (http://www.justice.gov/opa/pr/attorney-general -eric-holder-announces-revisions-uniform-crime -report-s-definition-rape).

United States Department of Justice. Bureau of Justice Statistics. "Female Victims of Sexual Violence, 1994-2010." March 2013. Retrieved August 5, 2014 (http://www.bjs.gov/content/pub /pdf/fvsv9410.pdf).

Vannier, Sarah A., Anna B. Currie, and Lucia F. O'Sullivan. "Schoolgirls and Soccer Moms: A Content Analysis of Free 'Teen' and 'MILF' Online Pornography." *Journal of Sex Research*, 51(3), April 1, 2014.

Vega, Cecilia. "Richmond Rape Witness Describes the Assault." ABC7News.com, November 12, 2009. Retrieved September 17, 2014 (http://abc7news.com/ archive/7111732).

INDEX

R

S

ABOUT THE AUTHOR

As a high school and college educator for over thirty years, Susan Henneberg has witnessed the devastating effects of sexual violence on teens and young adults. She is the author of numerous books on such topics as social media, career planning, and academic and personal success. She is a parent of three daughters and lives in Reno, Nevada.

PHOTO CREDITS